The Way Home in the Night

Akiko Miyakoshi

Kids Can Press

On our way home, we see the restaurant
and bookshop closing for the night.

My mother carries me through the quiet streets.

Most of our neighbors are already home.
I can see their lights in the windows.

I hear a phone ring. Who is calling?

Mmm … It smells like pie.

A light flickers. Maybe someone is watching TV.

And it sounds like there is a big party next door.

I look in a window and see someone saying goodbye.

When we are almost home, my father joins us.
Soon he will tuck me into bed.

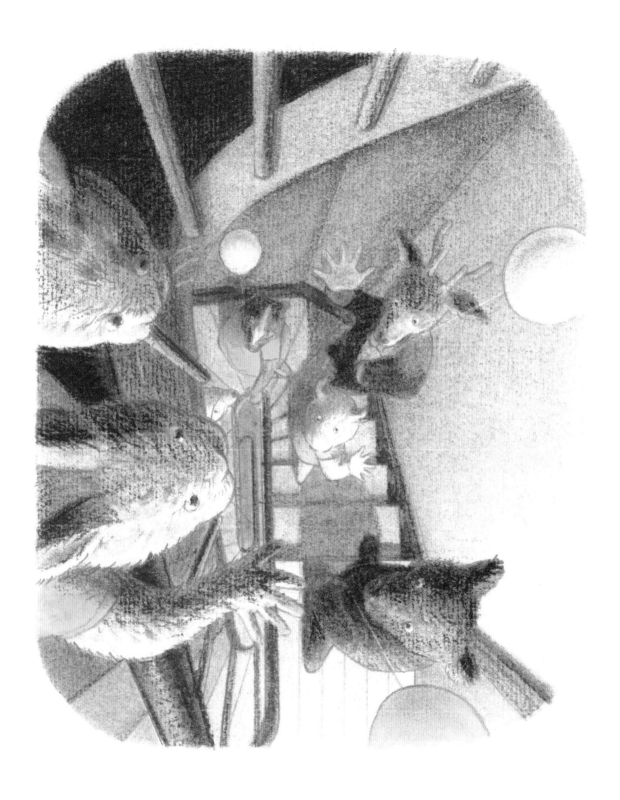

Snug under my covers, I think about the way home.
Are the party guests saying goodnight?

Is the person on the phone getting ready for bed?

Maybe the cook from the restaurant is taking a bath,

and the bookseller is reading on the couch.

Is the pie ready to be shared?

Have all the lights been turned off for the night?

As I fall asleep, I hear footsteps in the street.

I wonder if she is going to the station.

Will she take the last train home?

Some nights are ordinary,
and other nights are special.

But every night, we all
go home to bed.

Goodnight.

This edition published by Kids Can Press in 2017

Yoru no Kaerimichi
Copyright © 2015 Akiko Miyakoshi
First published in Japan in 2015 by Kaisei-Sha Publishing Co. Ltd., Tokyo
English translation rights arranged with Kaisei-Sha Publishing Co. Ltd.,
through Japan Foreign-Rights Centre
English translation © 2017 Kids Can Press

Kids Can Press gratefully acknowledges the financial support of the Government
of Ontario, through the Ontario Media Development Corporation.

Published in Canada and the U.S. by Kids Can Press Ltd.
25 Dockside Drive, Toronto, ON M5A 0B5

Kids Can Press is a Corus Entertainment Inc. company

www.kidscanpress.com

The artwork in this book was rendered in pencil, charcoal and acrylic gouache.
The text is set in Minion Pro.

English edition edited by Katie Scott and Yvette Ghione

Printed and bound in Shenzhen, China, in 10/2016 by C & C Offset

CM 17 0 9 8 7 6 5 4 3 2 1

Library and Archives Canada Cataloguing in Publication

Miyakoshi, Akiko, 1982–
[Yoru no kaerimichi. English]
    The way home in the night / written and illustrated by
Akiko Miyakoshi.

Translation of: Yoru no kaerimichi.
ISBN 978-1-77138-663-0 (hardback)

    I. Title. II. Title: Yoru no kaerimichi. English.
PZ7.M682Wa 2017   j895.6'36   C2016-902151-3